SANTA LAST TIME

Latonya Gaston L.S.G

SAMUEL
SANTA

SANTA GIFTS BAGS

SAMUEL SANTA KNEW THAT CHRISTMAS WAS AROUND THE CORNER AND HE WANT TO BUILD A CAR THAT LOOK LIKE A SLEIGH BUT FLY THROUGH THE STREET ON WHEELS. OF COURSE NOBODY EVER HEARD OF SUCH NONSENSE

THIS SLEIGH WAS NOT LIKE THE OTHER SLEIGH THAT WE HAVE SEEN BEFORE. THIS SLEIGH CAR WAS TOTALLY DIFFERENT.

SAMUEL COULD NOT HARDLY WAIT TO RIDE IN THIS CAR.

THE ONLY THING HE COULD THINK OF, IS THIS CAR COULD FLY, IN THE AIR, AND DRIVE, ON THE STREET. SAMUEL SAID, "THIS CAR MUST HAVE SOMETHING ABOUT IT, WHICH MAKE IT VERY STRANGE, BUT HIGHLY MAGICAL." SAMUEL SAID, "WHEN THE CHILDREN SEE HIM RIDING IN HIS SLEIGH CAR THROUGH THE AIR, THEY WILL IMMEDIATELY START LAUGHING."

CHILDREN LAUGHING LOUDLY

SAMUEL READY TO GET STARTED

SAMUEL WAS READY TO START ON HIS
NEW IDEA FOR HIS SLEIGH CAR.

SANTA STARTED BUYING HIS TOOLS AND SUPPLIES FOR THIS CAR.

EVERY DAY, SAMUEL WOULD WORK,ON THIS CAR, UNTIL DARK, AND NOW HE IS ALMOST FINISHED, THE ONLY THINGS WAS LEFT,WAS TO PUT ON HIS NEW TIRES.

★

SAMUEL SAID TO HIMSELF, "IT IS BEGINNING TO LOOK MORE LIKE CHRISTMAS." SAMUEL SAID, "WOULD YOU AGREE?"

NEXT TWO DAYS IS VERY IMPORTANT TO SAMUEL.

THE NEXT TWO DAYS WILL BE VERY VITAL, TO SAMUEL, BECAUSE HE WILL, NEED THIS TIME IN ORDER TO, GET THINGS DONE. AS SOON AS SAMUEL FINISHED HIS SLEIGH CAR, SAMUEL STARTED PACKING ALL THE TOYS IN A BAG FOR HIS TRIP ON CHRISTMAS EVE.

AT LAST THE BAG
WAS FILLED

ALL THROUGH THE CITY OF CHICAGO, ILLINOIS

KEEP IN MIND SAMUEL SANTA, WAS 65 YEARS OLD, AND IT WAS TIME FOR HIM TO RETIRE, BECAUSE HE WAS TOO OLD NOW TO CONTINUE TO PLAY SANTA. NOBODY KNEW, THAT THIS WAS, SAMUEL SANTA, LAST TIME, FOR DELIVERING, CHRISTMAS GIFTS, FOR CHICAGO, ILLINOIS.

PEOPLE DID NOT KNOW ANYWHERE, ABOUT HIS LITTLE SECRET, NOT EVEN HIS CLOSEST FRIENDS. SAMUEL WANTED, TO TELL THE PEOPLE, WHO HE WAS, AND WHY. SAMUEL ALSO WANTED TO TELL THEM WHY THEY WILL NOT, HAVE A SANTA CLAUS, NEXT YEAR, TO DELIVER THEIR CHRISTMAS GIFTS. SANTA SAMUEL KNEW THIS WAS HIS LAST TIME.

SANTA MAKE A BIG SIGN THAT EXPLAIN WHAT WILL BE HAPPENING NEXT YEAR.

THE SIGN WILL TELL THE PEOPLE, WHAT HIS REAL NAME IS, AND WHY HE IS RETIRING. THE SIGN WIL BE HUNG UP ON CHRISTMAS EVE, BEFORE SAMUEL SANTA DELIVER, HIS CHRISTMAS GIFTS, THROUGHOUT THE CITY, OF CHICAGO, ILLINOIS.

SAMUEL WROTE

HIS SIGN TO HANG UP.

AS IT GREW CLOSER TO 25TH OF DECEMBER, SNOW BEGIN TO FALL ON THE GROUND LIKE RAIN, AND FLAKES. NOW THE TIME HAS FINALLY CAME TO TEST DRIVE TEST HIS NEW SLEIGH.

SAMUEL SANTA DECIDED, TO TEST DRIVE, HIS NEW SLEIGH CAR, BUT THE ONLY PROBLEM IS, HE COULD NOT DRIVE AT NIGHT, WHEN THERE WAS PEOPLE WATCHING HIM OR IN SIGHT.

SANTA WENT OUT IN COLD SNOW FOR A MOMENT.

SAMUEL SANTA SAID TO HIMSELF SOFTLY, "IT IS SOMETHING DIFFERENT ABOUT THIS SNOW, NOT ONLY IS IT COLD, BUT IT HAS SOME, TYPE OF, MAGIC IN IT." SAMUEL SAID, "I WILL TAKE MY CAR, FOR A SLEIGH RIDE TONIGHT, WITHOUT ANYBODY KNOWING IT.

IT WAS NIGHT TIME, AND SNOW WAS ON THE GROUND.

SAMUEL WENT TO GET SLEIGH CAR THAT HE BUILT.

THE ONLY THING, SAMUEL COULD THINK OF, IS HOW FAST THIS CAR, WILL GO, IN THE SNOW. SAMUEL KNEW, HE HAD TWO DAYS LEFT, BEFORE IT WILL BE CHRISTMAS EVE. SAMUEL WALKED OVER TO THE SLEIGH CAR TO GET IN WITHOUT ANY PROBLEMS.

SAMUEL WAS NOW EAGER TO DRIVE, AND HE KNEW THAT IT WAS IMPORTANT TO GET THINGS DONE.

SAMUEL FINALLY GET READY

SAMUEL WAS FINALLY READY FOR THE MAIN EVENT ON CHRISTMAS EVE. HE KNEW THIS WOULD BE HIS LAST DELIVERY AND HE NEEDED TO MAKE HIS LAST IMPRESSION ON THE CITY OF CHICAGO, ILLINOIS.

TOYS ARE IN THE BAG

SLEIGH CAR AT NIGHT.

NOW THE TIME HAS COME, IT IS NOW CHRISTMAS EVE, SAMUEL IS READY TO LOAD UP HIS SLEIGH CAR FOR DELIVERY ON CHRISTMAS DAY.

SAMUEL SAID, "OH LOOK SAMUEL SANTA!!!!!!!!!!!!!!!!!!!!"

SAMUEL QUICKLY PUT ON HIS SANTA SUIT AND HIS BEARD ON. HE GLIMPSE IN THE MIRROR AND SADLY SAID, "THIS IS MY LAST DELIVERING, BECAUSE IM GETTING TOO OLD TO PLAY SANTA CLAUS."

SANTA FILLED THE BAGS WITH TOYS.

IT WAS FINALLY CHRISTMAS EVE, AND ALL THROUGH THE SNOW. SAMUEL WAS DELIVERING GIFTS THROUGH OUT CHICAGO. AND EVERYBODY KNEW, NOT A CREATURE WAS RESTORE, BUT A SLEIGH WITH LOTS OF TOYS, AND SIGN HANGING ON THE MAYOR DOOR ANNOUNCING HIS LAST DELIVERING FOR SANTA IN CHICAGO.

MAYOR OFFICE OF CHICAGO

SANTA SAID, "MERRY CHRISTMAS TO ALL IN CHICAGO"

Printed in the United States
By Bookmasters